WHEN
AUNT LENA DID THE Rhumba

Eileen Kurtis-Kleinman

ILLUSTRATED BY
Diane Greenseid

Hyperion Books for Children

New York

Printed in Hong Kong by South China Printing Company (1988) Ltd.

FIRST EDITION
1 3 5 7 9 10 8 6 4 2

Library of Congress Cataloging-in-Publication Data

Kurtis-Kleinman, Eileen.
When Aunt Lena did the rhumba / Eileen Kurtis-Kleinman;
illustrated by Diane Greenseid.
p. cm.
Summary: When her aunt, who loves Broadway musicals,
is confined to bed with a sprained ankle,
Sophie convinces the rest of the family to put on a show for her.
ISBN 0-7868-0082-8 (trade)—ISBN 0-7868-2067-5 (lib. bdg.)
[1. Aunts—Fiction. 2. Family life—Fiction. 3. Musicals—
Fiction.] I. Greenseid, Diane, ill. II. title.
PZ7.K96255Wh 1995
[E]—dc20 94-35489

The artwork for each picture is prepared using acrylic.
This book is set in 14-point Centennial Roman.

E
KUR

For all the Lenas I know and love
—E. K. K.

To Adrienne, and in memory of Alfred,
for all the musicals that filled my childhood
—D. G.

When my aunt Lena did the rhumba, Grandma said the whole house shook.

Aunt Lena taught me how to cha-cha and do the Charleston. "Sophie, you're a natural," she told me. "A born star if ever there was one."

Aunt Lena loved dancing and movie stars, but most of all she loved her Broadway musical. Every Wednesday, off to the matinee she'd go, leaving a trail of lavender-smelling perfume behind her. Later that evening, Aunt Lena's taxi would drive up in front of the house. I knew it would then be Wednesday matinee time for me, while I ate goulash in the kitchen for dinner.

"Oh, darling. Magnificent! It was absolutely magnificent!" gushed Aunt Lena as she flung open the kitchen door. She'd waltz around the kitchen, humming the music and acting out the romance between the handsome hero and the *bee-yoo-tee-ful* heroine.

"Whaddya talkin' about, Lena?" my uncle Dutch would shout from the dining room, where he and Uncle Solly were playing cards. "Dreamin' Lena. Where do you think you are? The Ziegfeld Follies?"

"They're just jealous," she'd stage-whisper to me. And for the grand finale, she'd put her hand to her forehead and pretend to collapse onto a kitchen chair.

One Wednesday, in the middle of a showstopping number, Aunt Lena slipped on a piece of cooked cabbage and landed, THUMP, right on her big rump. "Oh! Oh! I can't get up. Help me! Please!" she wailed.

"Don't move! Now listen to me! I'm your mother!" directed my grandma. "Lena, don't you move!"

Aunt Lena moaned, each moan a little grander, a little more pitiful. There I stood in the middle of the confusion, feeling a little scared and a little giggly.

As it turned out, Aunt Lena had sprained her ankle. "It doesn't hurt so bad, honey," she explained. "Mostly it feels like I'm trying to walk on a giant piece of sponge cake. The doctor says I got to rest until it gets better. Shopping, bingo, and the beauty parlor I can do without. But my Wednesday matinee! That's what I'll miss!"

Suddenly I got an idea, but I needed some help.

I tiptoed into the living room, where Uncle Dutch sat, buried in the newspaper. "Uncle Dutch," I said in my sweetest pretty-please voice. "Let's put on a show for Aunt Lena. If she can't go to her Wednesday musical matinee, maybe her matinee can come to her."

Uncle Dutch made annoyed grumbling sounds, so I tried Uncle Solly. "Uncle Solly," I said softly, "Grandma said your boogie-woogie bugle sent sailors and their sweethearts swinging from the rafters. . . . Does that mean you could play the music for our show and I could dance?"

Uncle Solly just said, "Sophie, be a good girl and get me some black-cherry soda." I hung my head and trudged into the kitchen.

"Grandma," I blurted out, "Uncle Solly wants some black-cherry soda, and Aunt Lena is very sad because she can't go to her matinee, and I want to make a musical show for her. Right here, right in her bedroom, to cheer her up. Oh, Grandma, won't you help me?"

"What would you like me to do?" Grandma asked.

"Well, maybe you can help me with my costume. I need a feather boa and many necklaces and long gloves and a big hat. Oh, and maybe we can do the Charleston and maybe the tango. And maybe we can borrow records and the Victrola from Mrs. Pinsky—then we could have music, too. And songs!" I exclaimed. "We could sing songs from Aunt Lena's favorite shows—"

My grandma started to laugh, a real big laugh. "Oh my gosh," she said, trying to catch her breath. "You remind me of Lena when she was your age. Your aunt Lena, my little girl, always cooking up something.

"Look, I'll make you a deal. You bring the soda to Solly and let me finish in the kitchen, then I'll meet you upstairs in my room to see what we can find in my wardrobe for your musical."

On the way, I made a quick detour to peek in on Aunt Lena. She was browsing through piles of matinee programs she kept in a pink hatbox next to her bed.

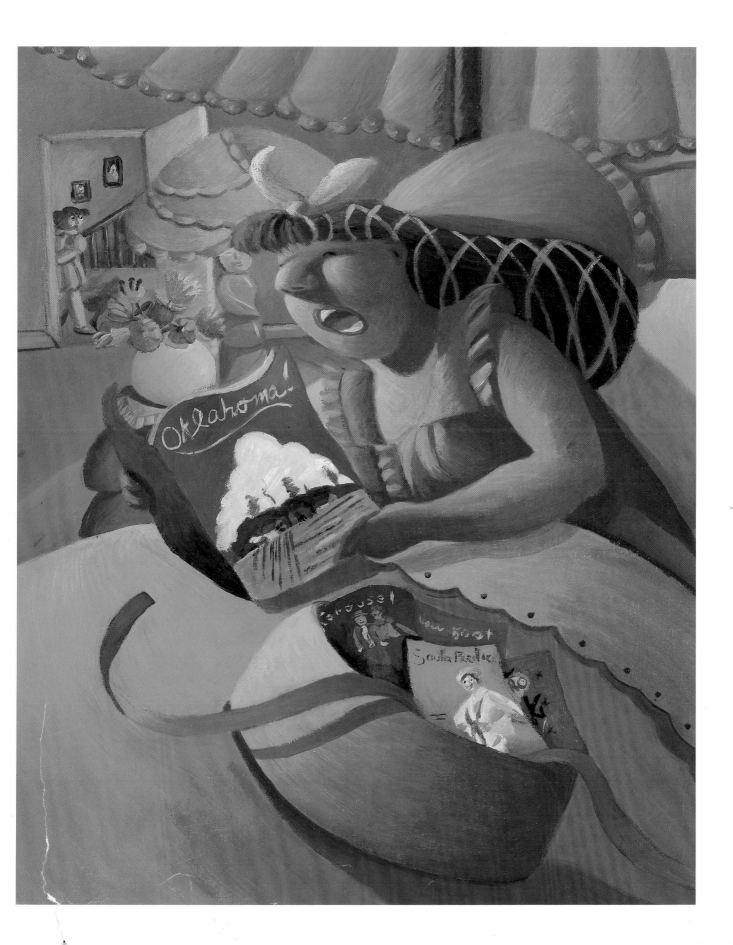

Half an hour later I appeared downstairs in the living room in full costume. Without a minute's hesitation, feeling like the showstopper Aunt Lena told me I would one day become, I belted out the first song that popped into my head.

"Take me out to the ball game. Take me out to the crowd," I sang with all the heart I could muster.

I swayed back and forth with hands on hips. Suddenly Uncle Solly joined in: "So it's one-two-three strikes you're out." And then Uncle Dutch sang along: ". . . at the old ball game!" He picked me up and danced me around the living room. My grandma came in to applaud us at the end.

"Oh, Grandma, aren't they *divine*?" I said, using one of Aunt Lena's favorite words. "Wouldn't it be great if Uncle Dutch and Uncle Solly could be in our show?"

"And why not?" my grandma answered with a mischievous twinkle in her eye.

Uncle Solly protested, "Aw, c'mon, leave us alone."

"No use arguing now, Solly. I *like* the idea," my grandma declared. "Tell you what, let's have a rehearsal in the kitchen while I look after my dinner."

The kitchen became our rehearsal stage. Every evening for the next few days, while Aunt Lena slept and my grandma cooked supper, we practiced our show.

Finally Wednesday arrived. As Aunt Lena napped, my grandma and I hung curtains made from old sheets in front of Aunt Lena's bed. I could barely hold still while we waited in the kitchen for our cue. Suddenly Aunt Lena's voice boomed from upstairs, "Hey, what's goin' on in here!"

"She's up," whispered my grandma. "Curtain time!"

Uncle Dutch led our chorus line. Uncle Solly circled around him, blasting his bugle. "Give my regards to Broadway. Remember me to Herald Square," we sang, with my grandma and me bringing up the rear, whirling tassels we'd borrowed from the living-room drapes.

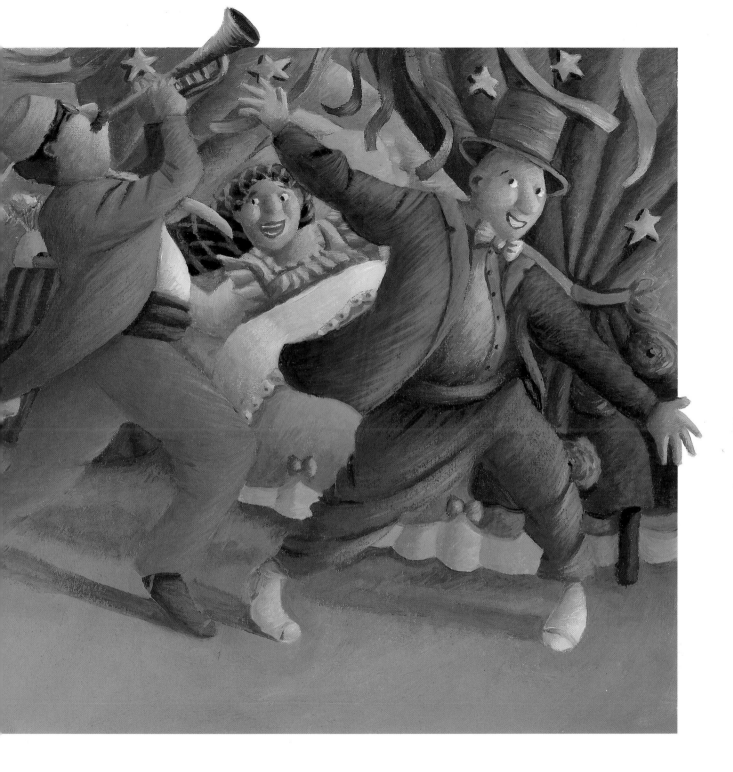

"Ladies and pussycats," began Uncle Solly once the song ended. "No, no, no," he continued, pretending to get very flustered. "I mean, babies and gentlemops. Welcome to Solly's Follies."

Uncle Solly began his medley of Aunt Lena's favorite show tunes while we all danced the fanciest, funniest steps we knew.

"Hey, Sol," called Uncle Dutch in the middle of one of our songs. Everyone froze and peered at Uncle Dutch. "What's worse than finding a worm in an apple?"

"I don't know, Dutch. What's worse than finding a worm in an apple?"

"Finding half a worm!" I burst in.

"Yaaaah!" said my grandma, sticking out her tongue, pretending to feel sick.

With that, Uncle Dutch and my grandma launched into a terrific tango. I followed across the floor, cheek to cheek with my stuffed dog Dolores.

Meantime, Aunt Lena chuckled, cackled, and applauded with great delight. "Encore! Encore!" she cheered as we took our last bow. Our show had made Aunt Lena laugh, and laughing seemed just the thing to help her get better.

Soon after, there I was, watching her wiggle into her purple matinee "number"—the name she gave to the special dress she wore to her Wednesday musical show. Suddenly she stopped, pointed her finger at me, and announced, "Get your patent leather pumps and pink pocketbook, honey—have I got a surprise for you!"

We walked down the busy street, hand in hand, people rushing past us. "It's almost curtain time," Aunt Lena said as she gave my hand a squeeze. We whisked into the theater and up the steps to Aunt Lena's balcony seats. As the lights dimmed and everyone grew quiet, Aunt Lena put her warm, perfumed arm around me and whispered, "Now, here's where the magic begins."